Sophie's Night Sky Adventure

by Jonathan Poppele

illustrated by Maria Lorimer

Adventure Publications

Cambridge, Minnesota

Acknowledgments

Special thanks to the team at Adventure Publications for making this book possible. Thanks to Maria Lorimer for turning my words into beautiful images and bringing this story alive. Finally, a warm thank you to "creative midwife" Rose Arrowsmith-DeCoux for helping me bring this story into the world.

Illustrations by Maria Lorimer

Cover and book design by Jonathan Norberg

Introduction

Stargazing is a magical activity. Looking up at the vastness of the cosmos can fill us with a sense of awe and connection—leaving us feeling very small and deeply comforted at the same time. For as long as human beings have been recording history, and probably for much longer than that, we have been telling stories about the stars. These stories have been passed down from one generation to the next since antiquity—an ancient tradition that continues today.

In this story, Sophie is introduced to some of the wonders of the night sky by her grandfather. The two of them sit out under the sky shortly after dark on August 10. The sky above them moves slowly over the course of the evening, as the earth turns. The sky changes hour-by-hour as the earth rotates, and it changes month-by-month as the earth orbits the sun. Most of the celestial objects that Grandpa points out to Sophie are called "circumpolar." Circumpolar stars appear to rotate around the North Star, or Polaris. They are always seen in the northern sky and are always visible above the horizon at mid-northern latitudes (including most of the United States).

Grandpa's cabin is located in the Upper Midwest, near Saint Paul, Minnesota. When looking at the sky from points farther south, a stargazer will notice that the stars and constellations appear closer to the northern horizon than they appear in these illustrations.

Late summer and early autumn are wonderful times to explore the night sky. The evenings tend to be warm, and the sun sets earlier than it does in June or July. If you head out stargazing at another time of the year, you will still be able to see most of the things that Grandpa points out to Sophie in this story, but they may have rotated to a different part of the northern sky and may appear upside down or sideways compared to what you see in this book.

I hope that this story inspires you to explore the night sky on your own and to share it with others around you.

— Jonathan Poppele

One warm, sunny afternoon in August, Sophie and her teddy bear, Max, piled into the car with Grandpa and Grandma to go to the cabin.

As they drove away from the city and as the sun dropped low in the sky, Grandpa began to tell stories.

He told legends of ancient kings and queens, fables of monsters and heroes and Olympian gods, and tales of great bears. Sophie sat mesmerized.

Being a bear himself, Max listened carefully, but he did not say anything.

When they arrived at the cabin, the light was fading and the sky was growing dark.

Grandpa turned to Sophie and said quietly, **"Let's go down to the lake. I have some old friends I would like you to meet."**

Sophie walked to the lake and onto the dock with Grandpa. As always, she carried Max with her. The air was warm, and the lake was as still as glass.

Grandpa spread a blanket out on the end of the dock and sat under the clear, darkening sky. Sophie sat beside him. For a long time, the three of them sat quietly, listening to loons calling in the distance and watching the stars appear.

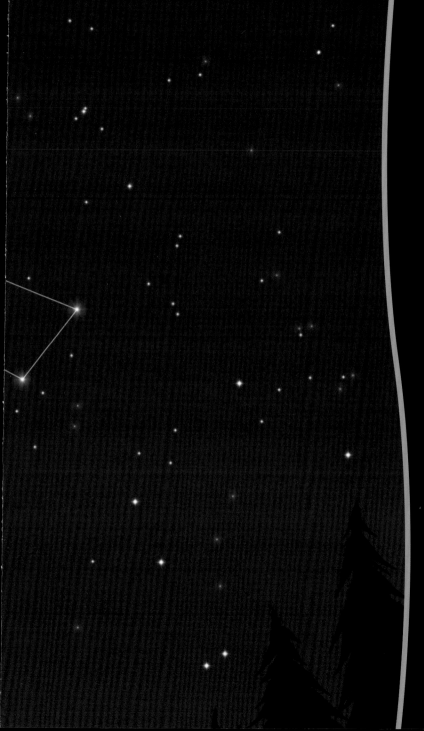

Grandpa leaned toward Sophie and Max and pointed up toward the sky. **"Do you know what that is, Sophie?"** he asked.

"It's the Big Dipper!" Sophie exclaimed. **"I learned about that in school."**

"That's right," said Grandpa. **"Did you know the Big Dipper is part of a constellation called Ursa Major? It means 'the Great Bear.'"**

Sophie and Max looked at each other in amazement. They had no idea that there was a bear in the sky.

He leaned even closer and traced Ursa Major. **"There is the bear's body, and that is its pointed face,"** he began. **"Those are the bear's long legs, carrying it across the sky."**

Sophie and Max sat in awe, following Grandpa's every move.

"And that," Grandpa continued, **"is the bear's long tail, stretching out behind it."**

Sophie looked puzzled. **"Bears don't have long tails."**

Max turned around to check his own tail, just to be sure.

Grandpa smiled. **"This one does, and it's a very special tail."**

**Can you find
Ursa Major?**

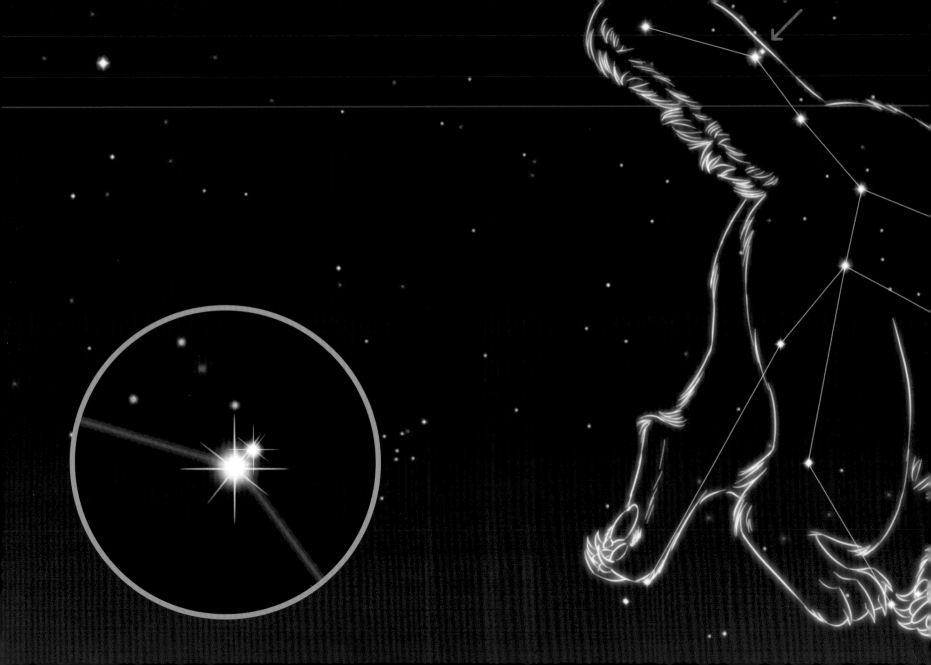

"Look closely at the star in the middle of the tail, Sophie," said Grandpa. "What do you see?"

Sophie looked for a long moment. The star looked just like all the other stars to her. Weren't stars all the same?

Then she spotted a faint point of light just above the bright star. "There are *two* of them!"

Grandpa smiled. "That's right. It's called a double star. Long ago, before there were eye doctors, people used those two stars as a vision test," he explained. "The bright star is called *Mizar* and the faint one is called *Alcor*. The name *Alcor* means 'the overlooked one.'"

Max thought that *Alcor* was a good name for the faint star. Even he had overlooked it at first, and he had excellent eyesight, for a teddy bear.

Can you find Alcor?

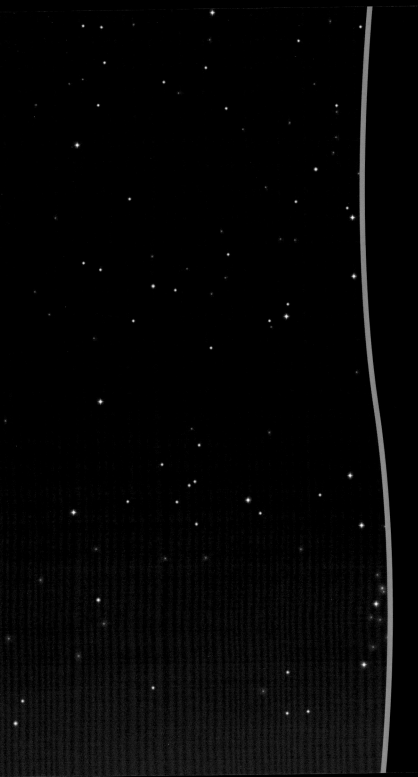

Sophie turned to Grandpa and asked, **"How do you find the North Star? Our teacher told us that you can find it using the Big Dipper, but I don't remember how."**

"Do you see the two stars on the front edge of the Dipper?" he asked. **"Follow that line to the next bright star you see. That's Polaris, the North Star. It's also the tip of the tail of Ursa Minor, the Little Bear."**

Sophie and Max perked up even more. **"Does the Little Bear have a long tail too?"** Sophie asked.

Grandpa nodded and traced the shape of Ursa Minor in the sky. **"Some people call those stars the Little Dipper,"** he added.

Max liked Ursa Minor. He didn't mind that it looked like a ladle.

Can you find
Ursa Minor?

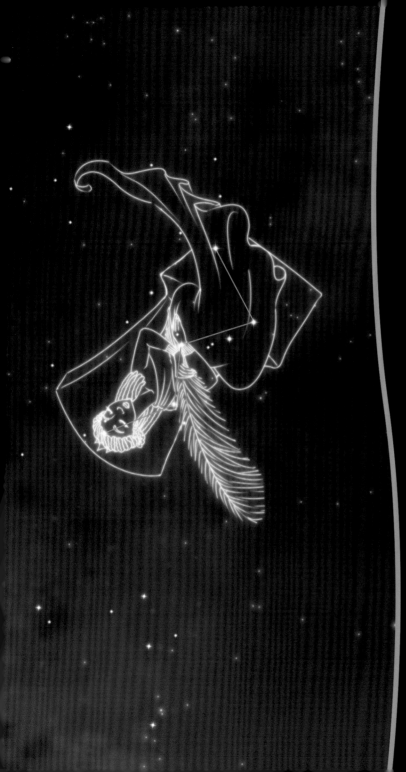

"**What else do you see in the stars?**" Grandpa asked.

Sophie looked back at Polaris, then off to the right, away from Ursa Major. There, opposite the Great Bear's tail, she saw a zigzag of bright stars. She pointed it out to Grandpa.

"**That's Cassiopeia,**" he said, "**the Queen of a land called Joppa. The stars make the shape of her royal throne.**"

"**I think it looks more like a letter W,**" said Sophie.

"**Most people do,**" said Grandpa, with a wink.

Can you find Cassiopeia?

Sophie noticed a band of faint white light that stretched across the sky. It looked kind of like a cloud, but it didn't block the starlight. She asked Grandpa what it was.

"That's the Milky Way," Grandpa replied, "the light of our own galaxy. Our sun is part of a galaxy, an enormous group of stars clustered together in space. The Milky Way Galaxy is shaped like a disk with a bulge in the center. We live out near one edge of the disk, so we see the rest of the galaxy from the side. That band is the combined light of billions and billions of suns. Long ago, the soft white light reminded people of spilled milk, so they named it the Milky Way."

After gazing up at the light of the Milky Way for a long time, Sophie asked, "Grandpa, are there other galaxies, or is ours the only one?"

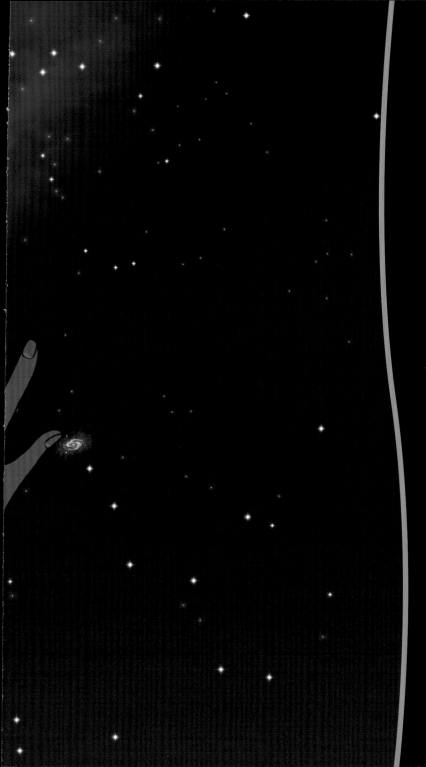

"There are more galaxies in the universe than there are people on earth," Grandpa replied. "Most of them are much too far away to see, but not all. Take a look at the three brightest stars in Cassiopeia. They form a triangle that points away from the North Star. Follow the point about the width of your hand, and you will see a small spot of light."

"I see it!" Sophie exclaimed. "It looks like a little smudge."

"That's the Andromeda Galaxy. It is made up of two hundred billion stars. It is the most distant object you can see with just your eyes. If we could ride on a beam of light, it would take us two-and-a-half million years to get there," Grandpa explained.

Max stared at the Andromeda Galaxy—the light of two hundred billion stars shining over two million light years away. He suddenly felt quite small, but somehow, he also felt comforted.

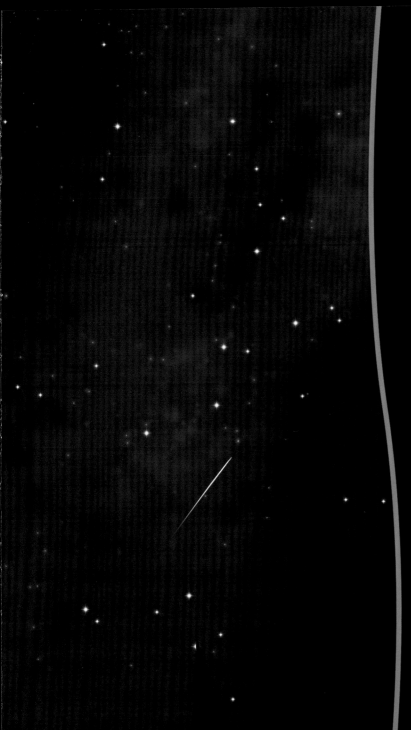

Just then, Sophie saw a streak of light between the stars of Ursa Major. **"What was *that*?"** she gasped.

"Some people call those shooting stars," said Grandpa, **"but they really aren't stars at all."**

"What *are* they?"

"Meteors," Grandpa replied. **"They are tiny pieces of rock and dust falling from space. They fall so fast that they burn up in the atmosphere."**

"Where do they come from?" Sophie asked.

"Some are pieces of asteroids," Grandpa said, **"but most are the dust left behind by the tail of a comet."**

Sophie looked back toward Ursa Major. **"That was a piece of a comet?"** she said, more to herself than to anyone else. **"Will we see more meteors?"** she asked Grandpa.

"We probably will. Tonight is the peak of the Perseid Meteor Shower. Early August is one of the best times all year to watch for meteors."

Max looked off to the east and saw another streak of light. No one else was watching. He felt very special.

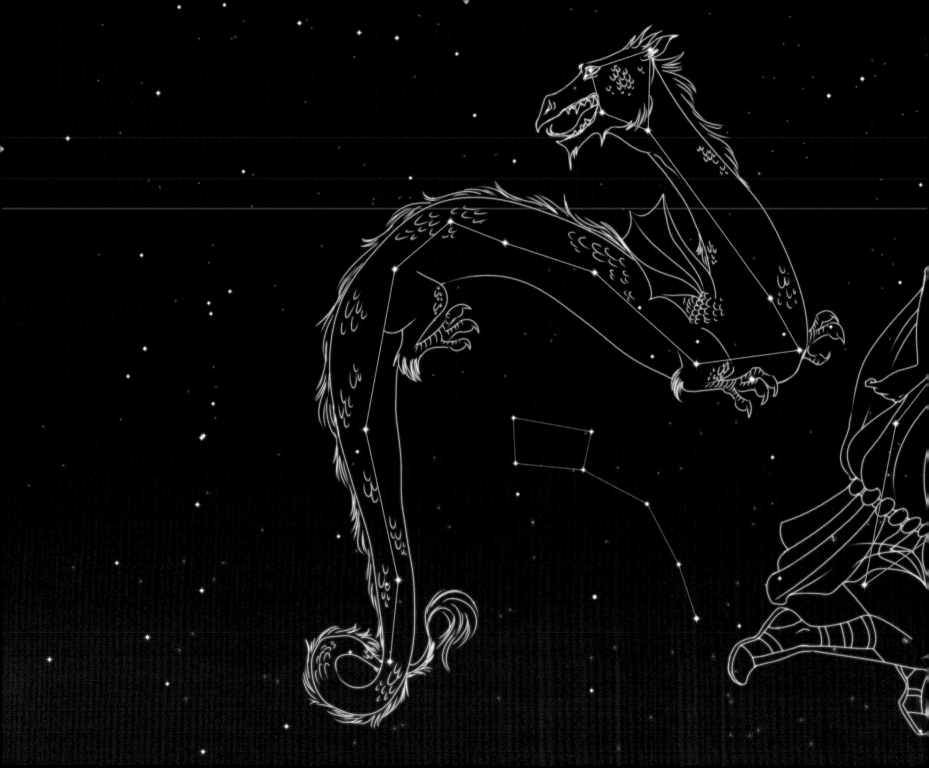

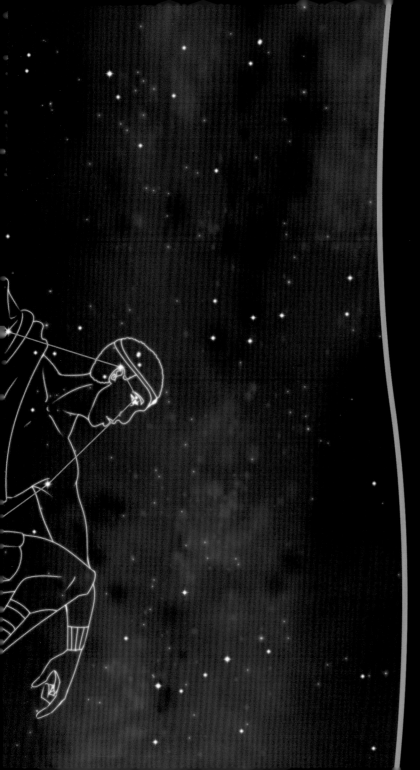

Grandpa, Sophie and Max laid on their backs and stared up at the sky. They watched for meteors while Grandpa pointed out more constellations.

"That one is called Cepheus, the King of Joppa. I'll say it again: SEE-fee-us. It looks like a cartoon house turned on its side."

Another meteor streaked across the sky.

"And that long string of stars, curving around Ursa Minor, is called Draco, the Dragon."

Sophie yawned. Bedtime was different at Grandpa and Grandma's cabin than it was at home.

"It's getting late," said Grandpa, **"but I have one more friend I'd like you to meet."**

Can you find
Cepheus
and Draco?

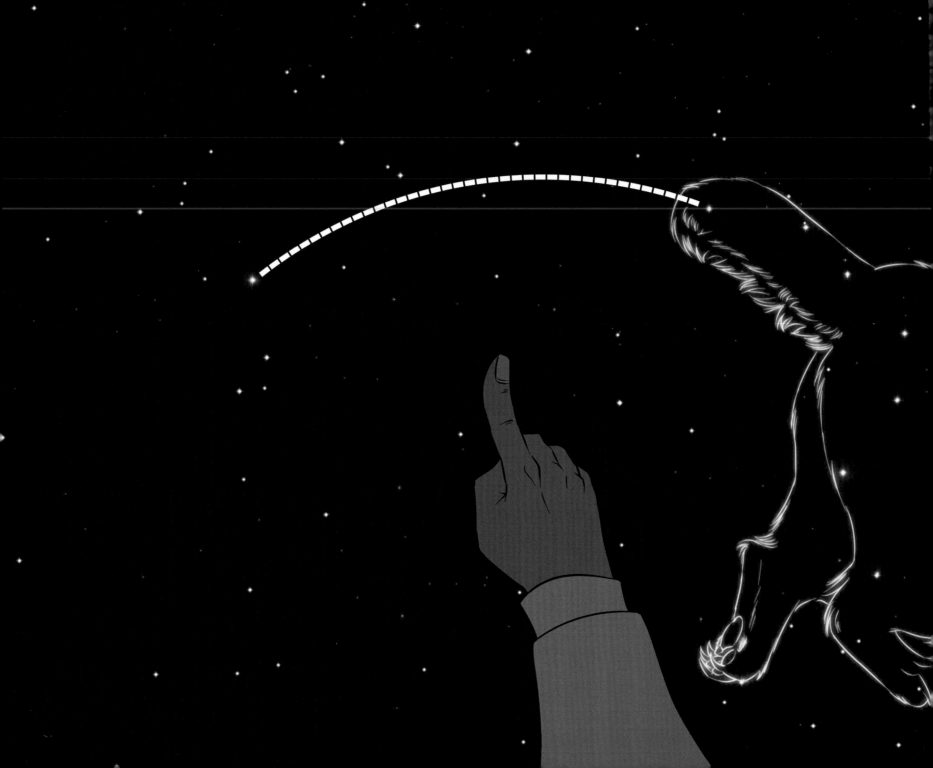

Grandpa pointed at Ursa Major. **"Follow the arc of the tail across the sky. What is it pointing to?"**

Sophie and Max traced the curve of the Great Bear's tail until they came to a bright orange star. Sophie pointed with delight.

Grandpa smiled. **"That's called Arcturus, the Guardian of the Bear. Every night, the bears march around the North Star. Every night, Arcturus keeps watch over them."**

"That's just like me, Grandpa," Sophie said proudly. **"I'm the guardian of a bear."**

Max agreed. Sophie was a very good guardian.

Can you find Arcturus?

They sat quietly for a long time, watching the stars. Sophie leaned against Grandpa's side and gazed at a sky full of queens and heroes and monsters and bears.

"You have great friends, Grandpa," Sophie said.

"Yes, I do," Grandpa said warmly.

Mythology

URSA MAJOR: The Big Dipper forms the most recognizable pattern in the northern skies. These stars are commonly known as part of the Great Bear.

In classical mythology, Ursa Major is thought to be Callisto, a beautiful young woman. The god Zeus fell in love with her, so Zeus's jealous wife, Hera, turned Callisto into a bear. Callisto's son, Arcas, grew up to become a hunter and saw a bear, which was really Callisto. Unaware of her true identity, he chased her. Seeing Callisto in trouble, Zeus pulled her into heaven by her tail, stretching it.

URSA MINOR: For centuries this has been one of the most important constellations, as it includes the North Star (Polaris).

One of the primary myths that's associated with Ursa Minor is also part of Ursa Major's story. The stars are said to represent Callisto's son, Arcas. Since Callisto wanted to be with her son for all eternity, the god Zeus changed Arcas into a bear. Zeus then placed Arcas into the heavens, along with his mother.

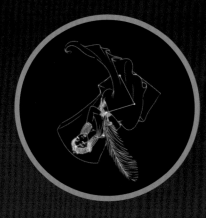

CASSIOPEIA: According to myth, Cassiopeia represents the Queen of Joppa, on the northern coast of Africa. Cassiopeia once bragged that she and her daughter, Andromeda, were more beautiful than the sea nymphs, spirit-like beings of the oceans. The sea nymphs complained to Poseidon, god of the sea. He punished Cassiopeia by sending a sea monster, Cetus, to destroy Joppa. (The story has a happy ending, though, as told in Cepheus's myth on the next page.)

Poseidon later placed Cassiopeia in the sky—but in an embarrassing pose. She is said to be seated in her throne, rotating headfirst around the North Star—upside down half the time—in eternal punishment for her bragging.

CEPHEUS: According to legend, these stars represent Cepheus, the king of the ancient land of Joppa. The god of the sea, Poseidon, sent a sea monster called Cetus to destroy the kingdom.

Cepheus and his wife, Cassiopeia, believed that they had to feed their beloved daughter, Andromeda, to the monster to save their kingdom. They chained Andromeda to a rock on the coast. She was saved by the hero Perseus, though. He defeated the monster and then married Andromeda.

It is said that Poseidon placed Cepheus in the heavens in honor of the tale.

DRACO: This ancient constellation is associated with nearly every dragon in Greek mythology.

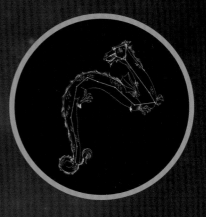

In perhaps its most famous legend, this constellation represents Ladon, a sleepless dragon with 100 heads. It was the guardian of a tree that belonged to the goddess Hera. The tree produced golden apples, which gave their owner eternal life.

The hero Hercules was forced to steal the golden apples from Hera's garden. Hercules defeated Ladon with a poisoned arrow and made off with several apples.

Saddened by the loss of her guardian, Hera placed Ladon in the stars. Later, when Zeus placed Hercules in the heavens, he put the hero's foot on top of Ladon's head, as a reminder of Hercules' victory.

About the Author

Jonathan Poppele is a naturalist, author and educator. He earned a master's degree in conservation biology from the University of Minnesota, studying citizen science, environmental education and how to cultivate a personal relationship with the natural world. He has taught ecology, environmental studies, biology, technical writing and composition at the University of Minnesota. An avid outdoorsman and student of natural history, Jon is a member of the Minnesota Astronomical Society and is the founder of the Minnesota Wildlife Tracking Project. A Black Belt in the peaceful martial art of Ki-Aikido, Jon is also the founder and Director of the Center for Mind-Body Oneness in Saint Paul, Minnesota. He can be contacted through his website at www.jonathanpoppele.com

About the Illustrator

Maria Lorimer has had a passion for art since she could pick up a crayon. Although she holds a degree in media arts and animation, she mostly dabbles in caricatures, comics and other cartoons. She is very proud of the fact that she can spot the constellations Orion and Ursa Major without any help. Maria is a lifetime resident of Minnesota and lives with her partner, her son, and far too many cats.